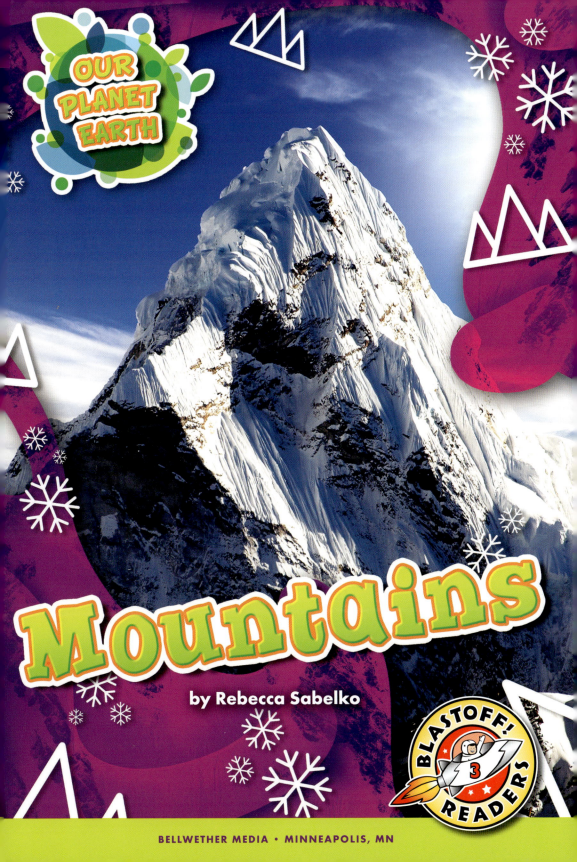

OUR PLANET EARTH

Mountains

by Rebecca Sabelko

BLASTOFF! READERS
3

BELLWETHER MEDIA • MINNEAPOLIS, MN

Blastoff! Readers are carefully developed by literacy experts to build reading stamina and move students toward fluency by combining standards-based content with developmentally appropriate text.

Level 1 provides the most support through repetition of high-frequency words, light text, predictable sentence patterns, and strong visual support.

Level 2 offers early readers a bit more challenge through varied sentences, increased text load, and text-supportive special features.

Level 3 advances early-fluent readers toward fluency through increased text load, less reliance on photos, advancing concepts, longer sentences, and more complex special features.

★ **Blastoff! Universe**

Reading Level

Grade **K**

Grades **1–3**

Grade **4**

This edition first published in 2022 by Bellwether Media, Inc.

No part of this publication may be reproduced in whole or in part without written permission of the publisher. For information regarding permission, write to Bellwether Media, Inc., Attention: Permissions Department, 6012 Blue Circle Drive, Minnetonka, MN 55343.

Library of Congress Cataloging-in-Publication Data

LC record for Mountains available at: https://lccn.loc.gov/2021045045

Editor: Kieran Downs   Designer: Laura Sowers

Printed in the United States of America, North Mankato, MN.

Table of Contents

What Are Mountains?

Mountains are landforms that rise high above surrounding areas. They are found on land and in oceans!

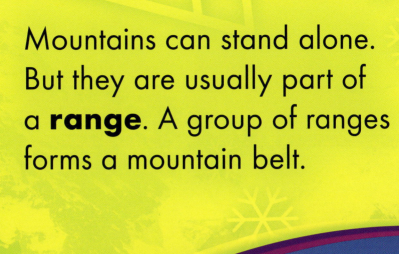

Mountains can stand alone. But they are usually part of a **range**. A group of ranges forms a mountain belt.

range

Mountains have different parts.
Peaks are mountain tops.
Some tall mountains have
snow lines.

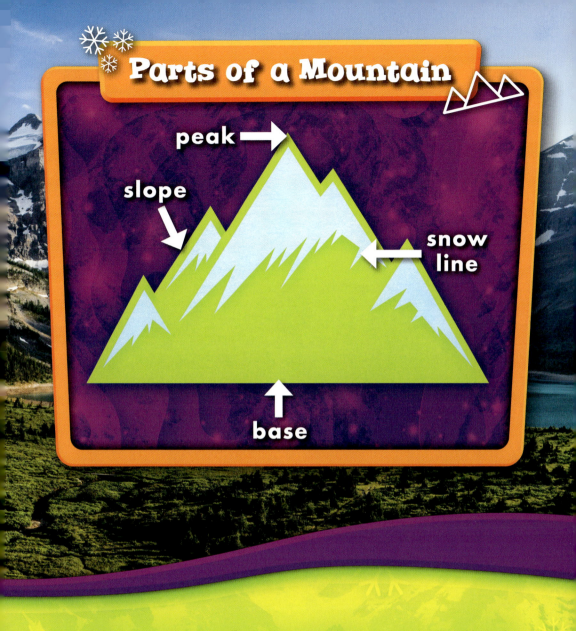

Parts of a Mountain

peak

slope

snow line

base

The sides of mountains are called **slopes**. Mountains meet flatter ground at their bases.

Changes in Earth's **crust** form mountains. **Fold mountains** form when **tectonic plates** push together. Rocks fold upward.

Mount Everest

Famous For

- World's tallest peak
- Part of the world's tallest mountain belt, the Himalayas

Height

- More than 29,000 feet (8,839 meters) above sea level

Type

fold mountain

Asia

Mount Everest, Nepal

fault-block mountains

Fault-block mountains form along cracks in Earth's crust. One side of the crack moves up. The other side moves down.

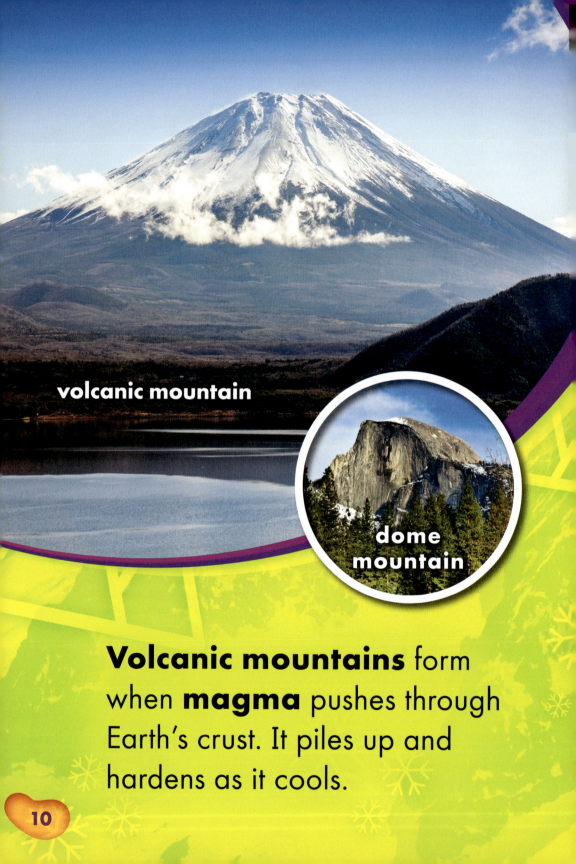

volcanic mountain

dome
mountain

Volcanic mountains form when **magma** pushes through Earth's crust. It piles up and hardens as it cools.

Sometimes magma does not break through the crust. It pushes rock upward. This creates **dome mountains**.

Mauna Loa

Famous For

- Largest active volcano on Earth
- Mauna Loa means "Long Mountain" in the Hawaiian language

Type

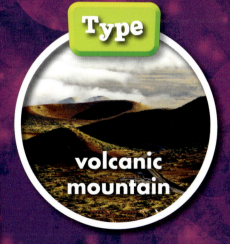

volcanic mountain

Hawaii

Mauna Loa, Hawaii

Size

- About 13,680 feet (4,170 meters) above sea level

Plants and Animals

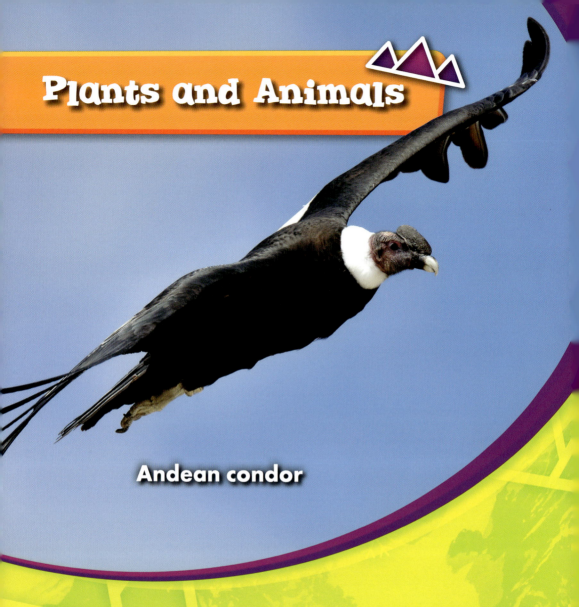

Andean condor

Many animals call mountains home. Condors soar between South America's Andean peaks. Tapirs feed on myrtle trees.

Bighorn sheep climb cliffs in the Rockies of North America. Bears roam through the lower fir forests.

fir trees

bighorn sheep

Chamois eat grasses in Europe's Alps. Gorillas feast on bamboo in East Africa's Virunga Mountains.

Mountain Animals

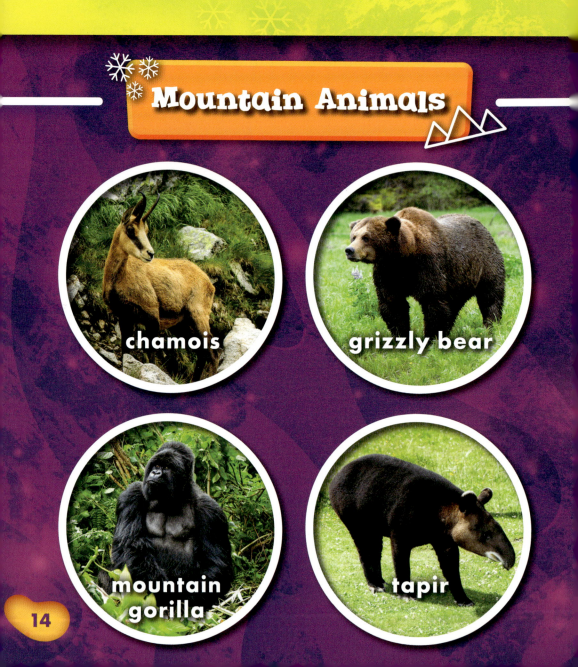

chamois

grizzly bear

mountain gorilla

tapir

snow leopard

Snow leopards go nearly unseen high in Asia's Himalayas. Snow trout fill rivers that flow down slopes.

Mountains are home to many things people need. Mountain rivers are used to create power.

People mine rocks and other materials. Mountain forests provide wood for building things. People also visit mountains for activities like hiking and skiing.

power plant
in the Rockies

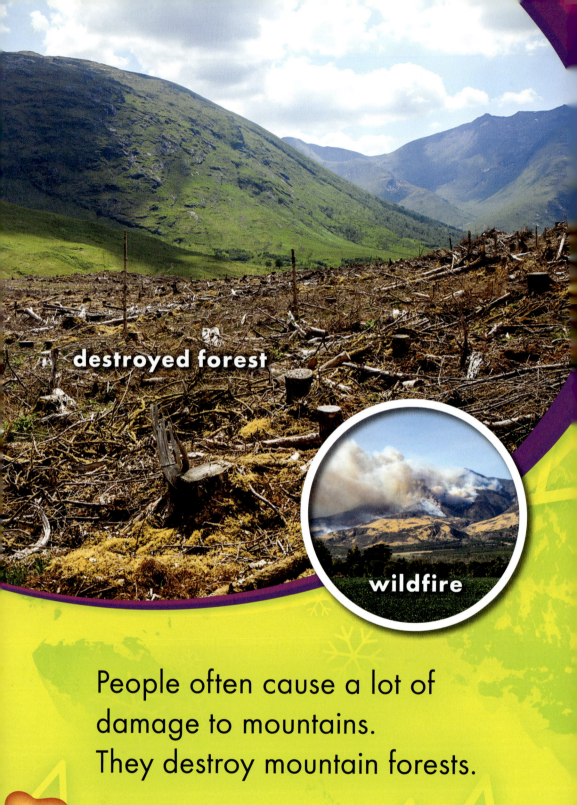

destroyed forest

wildfire

People often cause a lot of damage to mountains.
They destroy mountain forests.

Climate change affects the land. Wildfires become more common. Plants and animals struggle to survive in their changing homes.

How People Affect Mountains

- Overuse is destroying mountain forests

- Climate change causes wildfires to become more common

- Plants and animals are struggling to survive climate change

People must work together to keep mountains safe. It is important to reduce climate change. People can use less.

Businesses need to have more earth-friendly practices. Mountains can continue to be beautiful with a little care!

Glossary

climate change—a human-caused change in Earth's weather due to warming temperatures

crust—the outermost layer of Earth

dome mountains—mountains that have a rounded shape and are formed from magma pushing up Earth's crust

fault-block mountains—mountains that form from a break in Earth's crust that separates tectonic plates

fold mountains—mountains that form when two tectonic plates are pushed together

magma—melted rock beneath Earth's surface

peaks—the top parts of mountains

range—a line of mountains

slopes—sides of mountains

snow lines—areas on mountains that are high enough for snow to remain throughout the year

tectonic plates—layers of Earth's crust that move

volcanic mountains—mountains that form from a hole in the earth called a volcano; when a volcano erupts, hot ash, gas, or melted rock called lava shoots out.

To Learn More

AT THE LIBRARY

Green, Sara. *Rivers*. Minneapolis, Minn.: Bellwether Media, 2022.

Pettiford, Rebecca. *Mountains*. Minneapolis, Minn.: Pogo, 2018.

Topacio, Francine. *Creatures on a Towering Mountain*. New York, N.Y.: PowerKids Press, 2020.

ON THE WEB

FACTSURFER

Factsurfer.com gives you a safe, fun way to find more information.

1. Go to www.factsurfer.com.

2. Enter "mountains" into the search box and click 🔍.

3. Select your book cover to see a list of related content.

Index